With love to all the children and staff at Aspire Nursery - and most of
all to Vasilis. Thank you for the joy and inspiration.
- J.P

For Joe, I love you
- M.P.S

With thanks to Louise Jackson and Denise Johnstone-Burt

First published 2019 by Walker Books Ltd, 87 Vauxhall Walk, London SE11 5HJ

2 4 6 8 10 9 7 5 3 1

Text © 2019 Jane Porter
Illustrations © 2019 Maisie Paradise Shearring

www.walker.co.uk

WALKER BOOKS
AND SUBSIDIARIES
LONDON · BOSTON · SYDNEY · AUCKLAND

THE BOY WHO LOVED EVERYONE

JANE PORTER ILLUSTRATED BY MAISIE PARADISE SHEARRING

It was storytime. Everyone wriggled till they were ready to listen.

Dimitri was new at nursery. He leaned his head on Liam.

"I love you, Liam," he said.

Liam didn't know what to say, so he said nothing.

The teacher began the story.

It was about a dragon, a volcano

and a magic teapot.

At morning play, Dimitri found Sophie, Stella and Sue.

"I love you," he told them.

But they giggled and ran away.

So Dimitri went to the tree with the big heart-shaped leaves
and put his arms around it. "I love you, tree," he said.

The tree didn't reply.

Some ants marched past.

"Hello ants, I love you," said Dimitri,

but they kept on marching.

It was time for lunch. The food was good.
Berthe served a huge pile of pudding.

"I love you, Berthe," said Dimitri.

"You mean you love my custard!"
said Berthe.

That afternoon Dimitri said "I love you" to the class guinea pig,

the paintbrushes,

Big Andrew and Little Bea.

But they joked or blushed or turned away,
and the guinea pig just burrowed
in the straw.

At home time, Dimitri told the teacher that he loved her.

"Dear Dimitri," she said, "I know you do. I'll see you tomorrow."

Dimitri walked with his mum past the bakery, through the park and over the canal. On a bench sat an old man who looked tired.

"I love you, old man," said Dimitri.

"Who are you calling old?" snapped the man, and he pulled his coat tighter around him.

After that Dimitri
was very quiet.

At bedtime he whispered,
"I love you, Mum."

"And I love you, Dimitri," she said.
"You're my best, best boy."

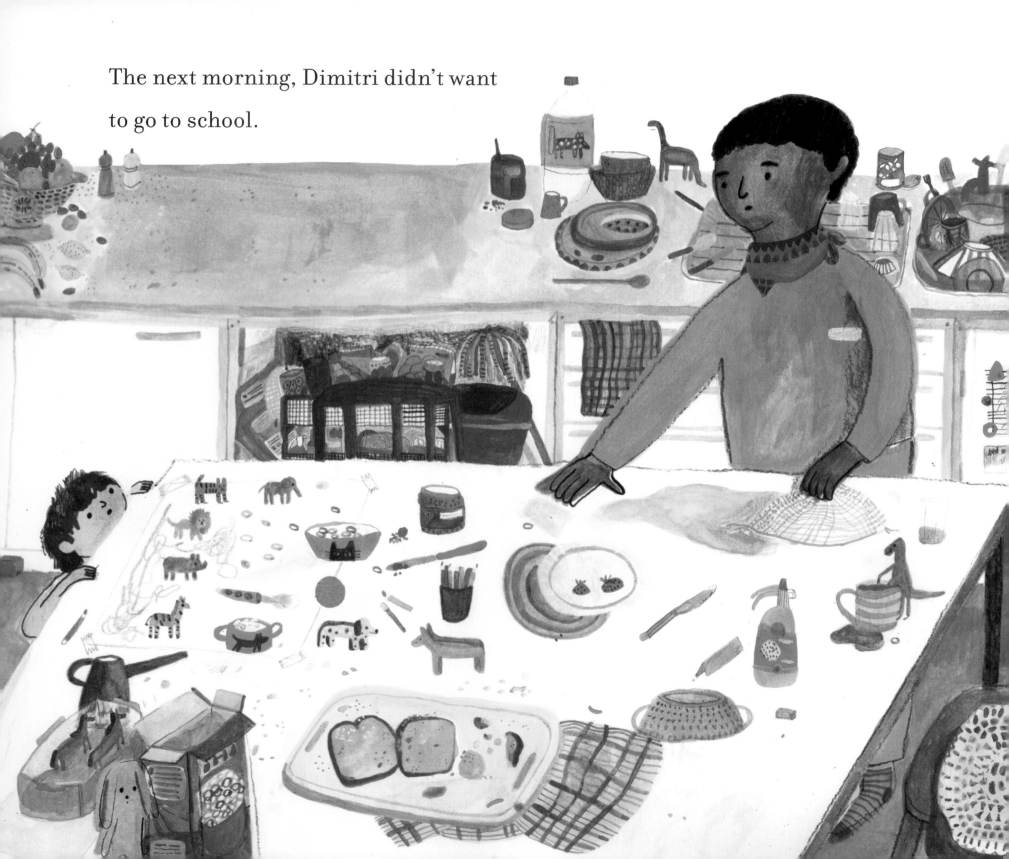

The next morning, Dimitri didn't want to go to school.

"I told everyone I love them, and no one said it back."

Mum helped him put on his coat and wrapped him up warm.

"People have lots of different ways of showing how they feel," she said, as they walked towards the canal.

"When you tell people you love them, they feel it, even if you can't always see it," she explained. "Your love spreads out and grows in new places."

They saw the old man on the bench. He was opening a tin of tuna and feeding the stray cats breakfast.

"You see," said Mum, "he's saying 'I love you' to the cats."

In the park they saw Berthe on her way to school,
and she gave a big, big wave when she saw Dimitri.

"Look," said Mum, "she's saying it with her smile."

The playground tree with the
heart-shaped leaves was filled with
singing birds as Mum said goodbye.
Beneath the branches, Sue, Stella
and Sophie were feeding the birds.
Dimitri looked at the tiny birds
hopping with enjoyment and
wished he could join
the girls.

He stood on his own, feeling
uncertain. But then Stella
saw him.

"Come and help us, Dimitri," said the girls,
and they gave him a packet of birdseed.
One bird jumped onto his hand and
tickled his palm with its lightness.

Then Liam came over and gave Dimitri a hug.

"Hello my friend! Will you sit with me at storytime?" he said.

A warm feeling started to grow inside Dimitri.

When they got to storytime, EVERYONE wanted to sit with Dimitri.
They made quite a pile. The pile made the teacher laugh.

"You funny children," she said. "I do love you all."

This time the story was about a frog, a mountain, and a rabbit
who loved everyone.

Even the guinea pig enjoyed it.